Rhode Island – A State of Firsts

1638
First Baptist church in America, founded by Roger Williams
First Baptist Church, Providence

1673
First and oldest tavern in America
White Horse Tavern, Newport

1763
First Jewish synagogue
Touro Synagogue, Newport

1772
First armed attack by American colonists on the British Crown
Burning of the HMS Gaspee, Warwick

1785
First and longest running Fourth of July Parade
Bristol Parade, Bristol

1793
First operating industrial mill in the United States
Slater Mill, Pawtucket

1828
First and oldest indoor shopping mall in America
The Arcade, Providence

1883
Oldest carousel in the United States
Flying Horse Carousel, Watch Hill

1909
Oldest continuously running Little Theatre in America
The Players at Barker Playhouse, Providence

1960
First automated post office in the world
"Turn Key," Providence

1978
First diner in the United States to be
included on the National Register of Historic Places
Modern Diner, Pawtucket

First Baptist Church

White Horse Tavern

Modern Diner

In memory of Doris Bahia Finelli, "Little Mama," April 23, 1924 – December 24, 2008. Growing up on the farms of Little Compton to living your married life in the renaissance city of Providence, you truly appreciated everything the Ocean State has to offer. — Mark Perry

To my quirky and wonderful home state of Rhode Island. What an excellent place to be from! — Lia Marcoux

Text copyright © 2017 by Mark Perry
Illustrations copyright © 2017 by Lia Marcoux

Produced and Published by Delor Francis Press
873 Atwells Avenue
Providence, Rhode Island 02909
www.delorfrancis.com

Typography by Inside Out Design www.insideoutdesign.com

Library of Congress Cataloging-in-Publication data:

Perry, Mark, 1974– author.
'Post' Mark—the North Pole postman visits Rhode Island / by Mark Perry ; illustrated by Lia Marcoux. — First edition.
32 pages   24.5 x 28.5 cm
SUMMARY: 'Post' Mark, the elf who works in Santa's mailroom, travels to Rhode Island to collect letters to bring back to the North Pole. Along the way, he learns about famous Rhode Island landmarks including: Slater Mill, Newport Mansions, Tennis Hall of Fame, Rhode Island Statehouse, Roger Williams Zoo, the Bristol Parade, and many others.
Audience: K to grade 3.
LCCN 2017938707
ISBN 978-0-9838947-3-5 (hardcover)

1. Rhode Island – Description and travel – Juvenile fiction. 2. Elves – Juvenile fiction. 3. Letter carriers – Juvenile fiction. 4. Santa Claus – Juvenile fiction. [1. Rhode Island – Fiction. 2. Elves – Fiction. 3. Letter carriers – Fiction. 4. Santa Claus – Fiction. 5. North Pole – Fiction.] I. Marcoux, Lia, illustrator. II. Title.

PZ7.P43535Posr 2017   [E]
                                        QB117-709

'Post' Mark –
The North Pole Postman
Visits Rhode Island

Written by Mark Perry   Illustrated by Lia Marcoux

DF

Delor Francis
PRESS

'Post' Mark, only a few letters and wish lists have arrived by mail from Rhode Island kids this year, and I need to get their toys ready for Christmas. Are there any more letters in the mailroom?"

'Post' Mark is the elf who works in Santa's mailroom and helps Santa go through all his letters.

"No, Santa, I haven't seen any," says 'Post' Mark. "Rhode Island is a really small state. I don't imagine there is much to do there, and not many letters would come from such a small place."

"Ho Ho Ho, 'Post' Mark! Yes, it may be the smallest of the 50 United States, but there are many fun things to see and do throughout Rhode Island all year long," says Santa.

"Can you please go to Rhode Island for me and collect letters from the children? I know they would enjoy seeing one of my elves and teaching you about the exciting places all over their state!"

"Start in Woonsocket to the north, and work your way south until you reach Westerly. Then, bring all the letters back to the North Pole so I can get their toys ready in time for Christmas."

"Rhode Island is famous for having delicious clamcakes and chowder. Can you please bring some back for me? Ho Ho Ho!"

3

'Post' Mark lands at Theodore Francis Green Airport in Warwick, Rhode Island. "Now, I need to find my way north to Woonsocket. I hope Santa is right and the children will be glad to see me."

'Post' Mark is very excited when he is greeted by hundreds of kids upon his arrival at the Museum of Work and Culture. Julia explains, "This is where you can learn about how many families moved to Woonsocket from Quebec to find a better life."

Aiden says, "Yes! That's true. People came here to work in the mills, but sadly many of the mill workers were kids who worked long hours and were not allowed to go to school."

When 'Post' Mark visits Slater Mill in Pawtucket, Carlos and Holly explain this mill also employed many children, just like in Woonsocket. "Luckily, child labor laws have been passed, so kids are no longer allowed to work in the mills," Carlos explains.

"This was the first operating mill in the United States and is a historic landmark with a working water wheel. It was built in 1793, and the wheel provided power to make thread out of cotton," said Holly.

"McCoy Stadium is also in Pawtucket and is home to Rhode Island's professional baseball team, the Pawsox," explains Michael.

"The Pawsox played the longest game in baseball history back in 1981," says Kaylee. "The game was 33 innings long and lasted over eight hours!"

"Wow! Santa is right!" says 'Post' Mark. "I have already seen so many fun things in Rhode Island, and still have more places to go! Plus, I need to find clamcakes and chowder to bring back for him."

"Welcome to Providence—Rhode Island's state capital and biggest city!" says Frankie. "The statehouse has the second largest marble dome in the United States," Maria explains.

"At nighttime, you can see and hear the crackling bonfires during our WaterFire festivals," says Frankie. "Italian gondolas are paddling up and down the Providence River while beautiful music is playing," says Maria.

"The Roger Williams Park Zoo is one of the oldest zoos in the country," says Kayla. Jayden explains, "Yes, there are over 100 animals here, and the zoo has helped protect animals that are endangered species."

Along Rhode Island's East Bay, 'Post' Mark arrives in the quaint town of Little Compton, which Doris explains is known for johnnycakes. "Johnnycakes are just like pancakes, but they're made out of cornmeal," says Doris.

Francis comments, "Yes, we grow the corn on our farm, and it is ground into cornmeal at the grist mill just down the street in Adamsville."

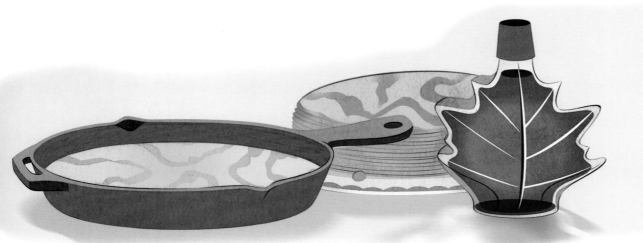

In the picturesque town of Bristol, Lisa explains, "We have the oldest and longest running Fourth of July parade in the United States."

"We are very lucky because Santa comes here twice each year," Manuel says. "In July, he marches in our parade, and in December he delivers all our Christmas presents!"

'Post' Mark says, "I am amazed there are so many fun things to do here year-round, just like Santa said!"

"Tennis anyone?" Annabelle asks. "Welcome to Newport, 'The City by the Sea.' Here you can see the International Tennis Hall of Fame and our famous mansions!"

● Exeter

Jacob explains, "The mansions were summer homes to many wealthy people from New York back in the 1800s."

'Post' Mark sees wonderful beaches in Narragansett. Max explains, "In the summer, we love going to the beach and swimming in Narragansett Bay."

Alexia adds, "The bay is home to many different kinds of fish and birds. There are even lobsters and clams!"

"Oh, so that's why Rhode Island is famous for clamcakes and chowder, like Santa was telling me!" says 'Post' Mark excitedly.

Newport

Narragansett

Block Island

Just below Narragansett Bay is Block Island Sound, where 'Post' Mark rides the ferry to Block Island. Mackenzie explains, "Block Island is only three miles wide and six miles long." Logan adds, "Not many kids live here during the winter, so we are very excited you are visiting the Block Island School!"

The Frosty Hollow Pond in Exeter is a trout-fishing pond at the Arcadia
Wildlife Management Area that is just for kids. "No grown-ups allowed!"
says Nathan.

"We also like horseback riding and mountain biking," Chelsey
explains. Nathan comments, "There are also lots of forest
animals living here, like deer, squirrels, and cottontail rabbits
too!"

Exeter

Narragansett

Westerly

"I finally made it all the way to Westerly like Santa said! This is so exciting!" says 'Post' Mark.

Emily explains, "The Flying Horse Carousel at Watch Hill is the oldest and longest running carousel in the United States." Austin adds, "Only kids can ride it, because the horses are suspended by chains, and not attached to the floor. So, the faster it spins, the higher the horses fly!"

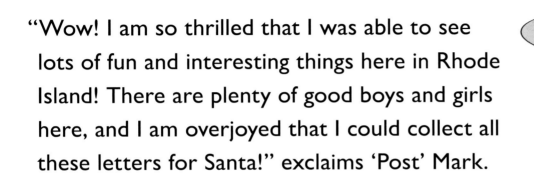

"Wow! I am so thrilled that I was able to see lots of fun and interesting things here in Rhode Island! There are plenty of good boys and girls here, and I am overjoyed that I could collect all these letters for Santa!" exclaims 'Post' Mark.

'Post' Mark stops in Warwick to enjoy clamcakes and chowder before arriving at the airport and flying back to the North Pole. "Santa is right. Clamcakes and chowder certainly are delicious! I can see why he wanted me to bring some back for him!"

When 'Post' Mark arrives at Santa's house to deliver the letters and tell him all about the exciting Rhode Island adventure, 'Post' Mark is very surprised. "Santa!" he exclaims. "I brought you clamcakes and chowder just like you asked. How did you get your own?"

"Ho Ho Ho, 'Post' Mark! I'm Santa! Remember, I see you when you're sleeping, and I know when you're awake. I was checking up on you while you were collecting my letters. You did a fantastic job, and I'm glad you had a great time visiting the Ocean State! Ho Ho Ho!"

FIRST BOOK ALSO AVAILABLE

'Post' Mark – Santa's Misfit Postman

As a young boy, Mark is deemed a misfit because his peers claim it is impossible to travel around the world and write stories about his adventures. Despite his classmates' taunts, Mark makes his way to the North Pole where he finds a place to "fit in" as 'Post' Mark—The North Pole Postman. In this empowering story, one learns if one holds true to one's beliefs, dreams can come to life.

This book may be purchased through most online book retailers, and at northpolepostman.com.

Visit northpolepostman.com

Visit 'Post' Mark's website to send your letter to Santa! Kids can send their wish list to 'Post' Mark, and he will forward it to Santa. Be sure to ask your parents' permission first.

Parents may also write to 'Post' Mark and tell Santa how their children are behaving or misbehaving!

'Post' Mark can visit YOU!

'Post' Mark loves to visit schools for storytime and entertain at Christmas parties. For more information, please visit northpolepostman.com.

NORTH POLE® POSTMAN

A Miracle and a Smile for Every Child